Philipp Winterberg   Nadja Wichmann

Io sono piccola?
Am I small?

AVAILABLE FOR EVERY COUNTRY ON EARTH
IN AT LEAST ONE OFFICIAL LANGUAGE

Italian (Italiano)
English (English)

Translation (Italian): Universal Translation Studio
Translation (English): Philipp Winterberg

Text/Publisher: Philipp Winterberg, Münster · Info: www.philippwinterberg.com · Illustrations: Nadja Wichmann
Fonts: Patua One, Noto Sans etc. · Copyright © 2016 Philipp Winterberg · All rights reserved. No part of this book may be
reproduced, stored in a retrieval system, or transmitted by any means without the written permission of the author.

Questa è Tamia.

This is Tamia.

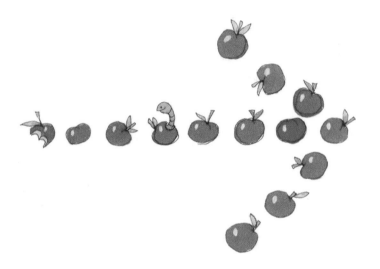

**Giusto!
Esatto!**

Right!
Exactly!

Tamia è ancora molto piccola.

Tamia is still very small.

**Io?
Piccola?**

Me?
Small?

Io sono piccola?
Am I small?

Piccolina? Tu? Tu sei piccolissima!

Teeny-weeny? You? You are mini!

Io sono piccolina?

Am I teeny-weeny?

**Piccolissima? Tu?
Tu sei minuscola!**

Mini? You?
You are tiny!

Io sono piccolissima?

Am I mini?

Io sono minuscola?

Am I tiny?

Minuscola? Tu?
Tu sei microscopica!

Tiny? You?
You are microscopic!

Io sono microscopica?

Am I microscopic?

**Microscopica? Tu?
Tu sei grande!**

Microscopic? You?
You are big!

Io sono grande?

Am I big?

Grande? Tu? Tu sei grandissima!

Big? You?
You are large!

Io sono grandissima?
Am I large?

**Grandissima? Tu?
Tu sei enorme!**

Large? You?
You are huge!

Io sono enorme?

Am I huge?

**Enorme? Tu?
Tu sei gigantesca!**

Huge? You?
You are gigantic!

Aspetta un attimo...
Ho capito! Io sono
tutte queste cose...

Wait a minute...
I've got it!
I'm everything...

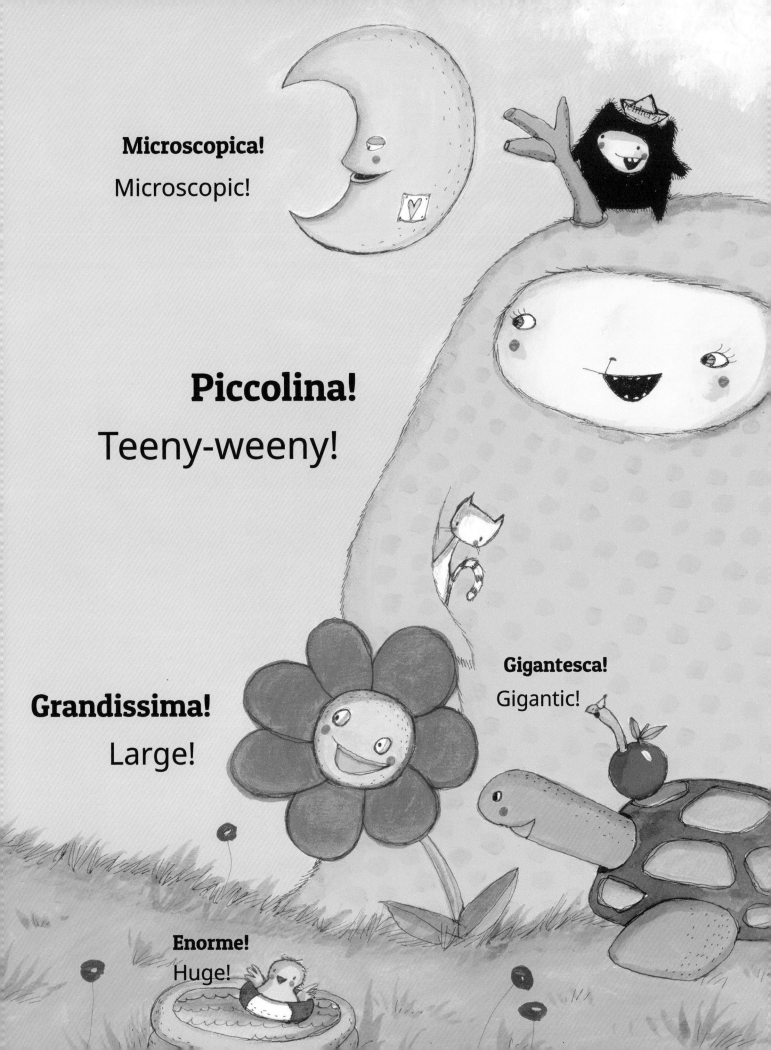

Microscopica!
Microscopic!

Piccolina!
Teeny-weeny!

Grandissima!
Large!

Gigantesca!
Gigantic!

Enorme!
Huge!

...e se sono tutte queste cose,
allora sono anche: proprio giusta!

...and if I'm everything,
I'm also: just right!

More Books by Philipp Winterberg

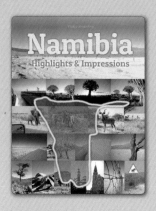

CPSIA information can be obtained at www.ICGtesting.com
Printed in the USA
LVIW01n2228181117
556706LV00003B/9